For Mabel Alice Waterfield x - M. R.

With love to the Goujons x – N. E.

PUFFIN BOOKS
Published by the Penguin Group: London, New York,
Australia, Canada, India, Ireland, New Zealand and South Africa
Penguin Books Ltd, Registered Offices: 80 Strand, London WC2R 0RL, England
puffinbooks.com
First published 2014
003
Text copyright © Michelle Robinson, 2014
Illustrations copyright © Nick East, 2014
All rights reserved
The moral right of the author and illustrator has been asserted
Made and printed in China
ISBN: 978–0–141–35073–8

Goodnight Pirate

Michelle Robinson

Illustrated by **Nick East**

PUFFIN

The stars are out,
the tide is in.
It's time for bed,
let's tuck you in.

Goodnight parrot.
Goodnight hook.

Goodnight spyglass.

Goodnight book.

Goodnight mainsail
and crow's-nest . . .

Goodnight Pirate

time to rest.

Goodnight cutlass.
Goodnight hat.

Goodnight cannon.
Ahoy, ship's cat!

Shiver me timbers!
There's an 'X'...

Drop the anchor.
Clear the decks!

To Treasure Island, off we go . . .

This way

Goodnight booty.
Goodnight shore.
Buccaneers for evermore!

Cutlass, cannon, book and cat.

Peg leg, parrot, hook and hat.

Scallywags
with
crooked
scars.

Flapping flags and moon and stars.

Goodnight ship

and treasure chest . . .

Goodnight Pirate, time to rest.